Survi
—vante

Translated from French

Survivor
Julie Guinand

Translated from French by
Rosie Eyre

First published by
Strangers Press, Norwich, 2022
part of UEA Publishing Project

All rights reserved
Author © Julie Guinand, 2022
Translator © Rosie Eyre, 2022

Printed by
Swallowtail, Norwich

Series editors
Nathan Hamilton & Lucy Rand

Editorial assistance
Lily Alden, Erin Maniatopoulou and Emma Seager

Proofread by
Senica Maltese

Cover design and typesetting
Glen Robinson (aka GRRR.UK)

Design Copyright © Glen Robinson, 2022

The rights of Julie Guinand to be identified as the author and Rosie Eyre to be identified as the translator of this work have been asserted in accordance with the Copyright, Designs and Patents Act, 1988. This booklet is sold subject to the condition that it shall not, by way of trade or otherwise, be lent, resold, hired out, stored in a retrieval system, or otherwise circulated without the publisher's prior consent in any form of binding or cover other than that in which it is published and without a similar condition including this condition being imposed on the subsequent purchaser.

ISBN: 978-1-913861-46-9

Translated by Rosie Eyre

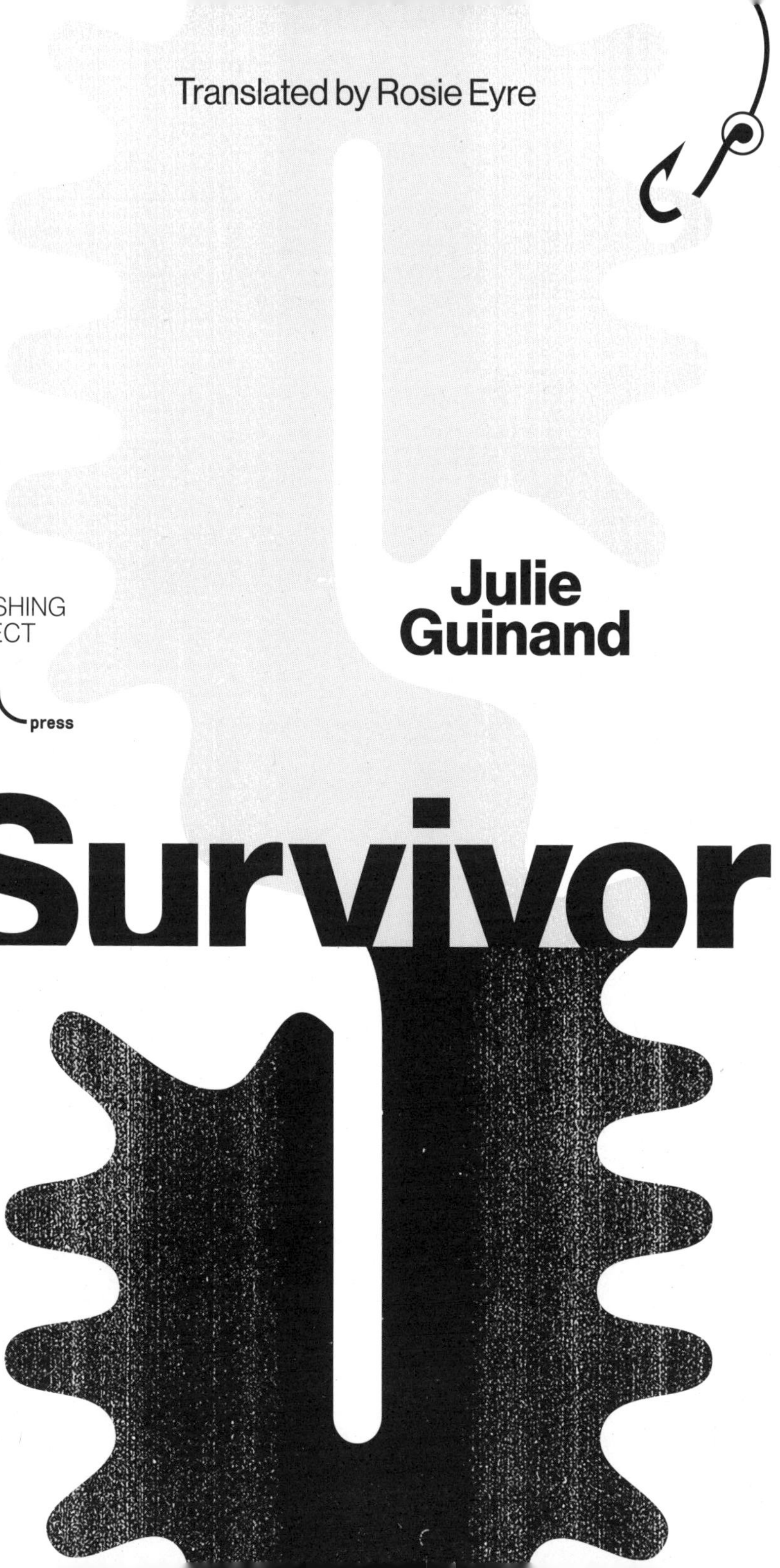

JEA
PUBLISHING
PROJECT

press

Survivor

Julie Guinand

DAY 1

DARKNESS. Without a crackle or flicker of warning, the living room cuts from yellow to black. I put down my book and grope for the lamp on the side table. More on autopilot than in optimism, I press at the switch. Click-click-click. No response. The bulb is already cold against my finger pads.

In the ten months since we moved to Maison-Monsieur, there have been four, maybe five power cuts. No biggie, then. But as I press away like a nutter at the lamp switch, my heart can't help staggering ever so slightly.

I stand up to try the big light. No joy. Bloody typical, just when my book was hotting up as well. I fumble for my phone, tap it into torch mode and venture out into the hallway. Through the oversized windows I can see the Doubs. Its glassy surface glints as the clouds drift by. The restaurant next door is bathed in darkness. But I know the neighbours have closed up for a fortnight. We got together for drinks before they left, toasting the Bahamas and the start of spring. I suddenly feel chilled to the core.

The fuse box is at the front of the house, in the cubbyhole that serves as a downstairs loo. The previous owner has diligently decrypted the maze of trip switches. 1-3: kitchen; 4-6: washing machine; 7: central heating; 8-9: upstairs and loft; 10-11: ground floor; 19-24: outside lights. I slide the ground floor switches back into the 'down' position, hold my breath, then race to the living room to test the light. Nada. And the sixteen others around the house? I tear up and down, from the basement to the loft and back again, panic setting in. My world has been pitched into darkness and it's too late to ring the electrician.

I root out this old diary. Hello again, old thing. I haven't felt such an overwhelming urge to write for years. I pile on three jumpers, one after the other, and burrow under my duvet.

DAY 2: I wake up full of beans, flick the light switch, and clock once more that it's a waste of time. Still, I won't let that put a dampener on things. I've a long day ahead and it will take more than a poxy power cut to put me behind schedule. Last night's panic seems overblown in the light of day.

My phone's displaying 'No Service'. Weird. I reach for the landline and punch in the number for the electrician. No dial tone. I pretend not to notice. 'Hello, *you!* How are things?' I boom into the receiver, laughing as I hang up.

My buoyant mood survives further silent treatment from the coffee machine, the printer and my phone charger. But it dies the second I open the fridge to fill the gaping hole in my stomach: mopping up an inch of standing water is enough to push me over the edge.

This outage couldn't have come at a worse time. I've got a big report due at the end of the week and I was planning on booking my plane tickets for Japan, tackling the unanswered emails in my inbox, sending out invitations for my birthday, calling my parents and paying off my credit card bill.

I fritter away the afternoon opening and closing Word documents on my laptop, without typing a single line.

DAY 3: I resist the temptation to open my web browser, oddly convinced the cybersphere is better off without me — as if my fingers, my thoughts or my negative energy were somehow responsible for cocking up the electrics, and the same could still be prevented from happening with the internet, as long as I keep my distance...

It's hard enough to contemplate life with no hot showers, no gratins bubbling in the oven, no bedtime reading, no playlists of corny French songs. But the prospect of life without Netflix marathons, without Skype, without compulsively checking the weather forecast, without emails from you... how do I even start to fathom that?

I spend all day like this, my index finger hovering over the mouse.

P.S. I cracked in the middle of the night. Feeling my way down the spiral staircase that connects my bedroom to the living room, I booted up my laptop and clicked the Firefox icon. *Oops, something went wrong. Please try again later.* The words reduced me to tears.

DAY 4: Today it's officially Back To Business. Time to restore some semblance of routine and productivity. I finish typing up my report, which drains the remaining battery. No matter. Racking my brains to remember the last emails I received, I draft replies on paper, then fill wads of Post-it notes with to-do lists for when the power comes back. I dig out an old road map of Japan and sketch a route from north to south, before eating a few dry crackers and pumping up the tyres of my electric bike.

Every twenty minutes, I check the landline for signs of life.

True, I could whiz up the Côtes-du-Doubs road to La Chaux-de-Fonds. I'd be there within half an hour. I could find someone to come and restore the power supply to this god-forsaken place. But that would throw me off schedule.

DAY 5: My power-less life is a sequence of blunders. I go through the same old motions, without distinguishing between those that still serve a purpose and those that have lost all sense. I flick the light switch as I enter the bathroom, set down the kettle on the perpetually cold stove, check my unresponsive phone, open and close the fridge door, press my hands to the radiator in the hope of gleaning some warmth. Occasionally I find myself chuckling at these reflexes.

I've Mum to thank for the jarloads of pickled veg sent when we moved in. I think of her while troughing them by the forkful, straight from the jar. Distress with a tang of curry. I check the phone again.

I keep putting off the trip into town. What exactly am I afraid of?

N.B. A list of genius inventions (which didn't seem like anything special before):

- the hoover
- the dishwasher
- the hi-fi (!)
- the fridge
- the oven (!!)
- radio
- hot water (! ! !)

DAY 6: Wrung out, I drift through the house aimlessly. Devoid of hope.

It's Sunday today. By my reckoning, the odds of the power returning on a Sunday are close to nil. Monday, though, seems like a fitting day for order to be restored. I cling to this.

DAY 7: Still no power, no light, no hot water, and not the faintest trace of signal. Something's wrong.

The neighbours are due back today. I station myself by the side of the main road, eagle-eyed. Not only does their Honda fail to materialise, but it dawns on me that there are no cars at all. Even though it's a Monday, and at this time there's usually a steady stream of through-traffic arriving from France.

For the first time since the power went, I'm struck by the dense, almost total silence.

It's a week since I last saw another human being.

At 8.00 p.m. I trudge back to the banks of the Doubs, stopping briefly on my way home to check for post. All the letterboxes are empty.

P.S. Before, I couldn't have told you whether toilets ran on electricity or not. I'm relieved to confirm they don't.

DAY 8: When did the birds stop singing?

DAY 9: I'm not a natural pessimist, but I have occasionally pondered what would happen in an apocalypse. How I'd react, what new reserves of strength I might discover, how far my survival instinct would push me.

I imagined a lot of things: the initial shock and ensuing daze, the cold, silence, fear and emptiness.

I imagined a lot of things, but not this: my stomach swarming with the same butterflies as the first time I fell in love.

DAY 10: A punishing day.

Waves of panic and fits of tears. My stomach growling even though I have no appetite. Bouts of nausea.

And despite my three jumpers and two duvets, this bone-chilling cold.

DAY 11: My ears keep playing tricks on me. I hear my phone vibrating, the doorbell ringing, footsteps on the stairs. I hurtle to the kitchen at the summons of the kettle whistling in my head.

Yet the facts are incontrovertible. There's nothing but thick silence and the crackling of logs that I burn through like a chain-smoker to thaw the ice inside me.

P.S. I woke up shrieking. In my dream, I was wandering the streets of a burnt-out town when I saw it smouldering in the embers. My father's hand.

DAY 12: I had fixed ideas about the end of the world (inspired by the disaster films I gorged on as a teenager). For example: it could only happen in New York, at night, and — god knows why — at the weekend. Also there'd be skies laden with black clouds, flashes of lightning, an earthquake, sirens, collapsed roads and buildings, wailing.

Here, everything is a picture of calm. The five buildings that make up the hamlet of Maison-Monsieur, of which just two are occupied, stand perfectly erect. The road, though deserted, still snakes along overhead. The forest around me is turning green, the Doubs is rippling ever so gently in the breeze, and the sky is feathered with clouds.

Have I made it all up?

P.S. I can't bring to mind my parents' faces anymore. I refuse to open the album. Seeing you there in the family photos might break me.

DAY 13: In my end-of-the-world fantasy, the characters reveal hidden depths and boundless ingenuity. The whip-smart gang fuel up their 4x4 with a jerrycan they find in the basement (evidently, transport plays a big role in this fictional apocalypse...) They scour the forest for a plant that will stem the bleeding of their injured child; uncover an old bunker and cram it to the rafters with tinned food; load up an ancient shotgun and teach themselves to hunt (my fantasy version clearly isn't short on military action either...). They know instinctively how to craft a splint from birch bark, or a lightning rod from two ends of sheet metal.

As for me, I don't leave my bed unless I need to haul myself to the loo or salvage a lump of flacid Gruyère from the lukewarm fridge (and steering well clear of the other rank offerings).

DAY 14: In my imaginary apocalypse, 'survival mode' kicks in from day one. The characters swing straight into action, hatching plans to gather provisions and set up a base camp, and driving the length and breadth of the country (in their 4x4) to survey the devastation or outrun a killer epidemic. Everything is filmed in breathtakingly beautiful panoramic sweeps.

My mental camera can only muster a single, out-of-focus shot, in greyscale, staring down the barrel of my inner world: the sense of dread at nightfall, my knotted stomach and trembling hands, the jerking beat of my heart.

DAY 15: Reasons why Maison-Monsieur isn't the worst place to live out an apocalypse:

- the house is partly wood-heated and both stoves still work
- it's literally out in the sticks (so no risk of running out of wood)
- the tap water is sourced from a nearby stream
- there are no other houses for miles (so lower risk of epidemics)
- the Doubs is swimming with fish (if you know how to catch them)

In reality I'm still languishing in bed, subsisting on whatever I can get my hands on (biscuits, spoonfuls of jam, tomato purée, tinned sweetcorn, curry paste, capers, olives, crackers), gulped down at ungodly hours.

DAY 16: I wake up seething, rage flaring from my lungs and engulfing the room around me.

Which son of a bitch pulled the plug on everything?

I use the term deliberately here, because in my view (biased, but scientifically sound), the apocalypse-maker can only be a man. He'll go by the name of Patrick, or Bob, or Jacques. And when Patrick/Bob/Jacques brought down the internet and power supply in one fell swoop, he won't have said 'oops' or 'shit', or – god forbid – 'sorry'. It'll be 'who fobbed me off with a crappy system like this?'

This apocalypse really couldn't have come at a worse time (have

I already mentioned? I think I might have). My career was really taking off. I was on the brink of securing a writing contract. A journalist wanted to do a feature on me.

    Has P/B/J put a stop to all that?

DAY 17: My wrath shows no signs of abating. Among its chief targets:

- the sun which still shines away like everything's fine
- interminable days of stretched-out agony
- whoever invented electricity in the first place
- my old physics teacher, who neglected to teach me the basics
- my laptop that won't turn on
- the stove that's giving up the ghost
- my no-show neighbours
- my family, who aren't showing any sign of life
- you, for not being my ever-present rock
- me, for being unable to drag myself out of bed

DAY 18: What am I being punished for?

    Since moving to Maison-Monsieur to lead a simple life, I haven't asked anything of anyone. I don't own a car or a smartphone, haven't flown in a decade. I recycle my rubbish, raise worms for composting, turn out all the lights before bed. I never take baths. I harvest rainwater.

    The apocalypse should only strike the polluters, the people who don't give a damn, the baddies.

    The likes of Patrick, Bob… Jacques.

DAY 19: Things I'd be willing do to bring back the electricity:

- donate an organ
- renounce all my earthly possessions
- cut five years off my life expectancy (?)
- lop off a finger or two (from my left hand)
- surrender the power of speech
- go teetotal

DAY 20: Mental note to P/B/J (9:33 a.m.):
Go fuck yourself.
Mental note to P/B/J (1:56 p.m.):
Right, guys, you've had your fun.
Mental note to P/B/J (9:12 p.m.):
Please, please, please, will you turn the power back on?

DAY 21: There's a *before* and an *after*. That's something I'm learning.

I can/must wave goodbye to that grant, my contract, the profile piece in the regional paper.

I can/must draw a line under evenings in front of the telly (halfway through the final season of *Jane the Virgin*, talk about a pain in the...)

I must learn to live without hot showers, lights, ice cream and music (no music!).

I must rewrite my existence.

DAY 22: I find myself gravitating towards 'feel-good' activities. So far, I've found a grand total of three:

※ belting out France Gall's Débranche in the huge kitchen
※ doing jigsaws
※ filling out sudoku grids

DAY 23, 24, 25, 26: ACTIVITY LOG
    Sudoku – jigsaw – jigsaw – singing – jigsaw – sudoku – jigsaw
    The hours have a treacly consistency. The only way of making life bearable is to take things minute by minute, one jigsaw piece at a time.

P.S. I wake up every night at 11:35 p.m. Why? I've not had another nightmare, I don't need the loo, there's nothing else to disturb me. I open my eyes, light a match to confirm that it's 11:35 p.m., then fall back to sleep.

DAY 27: Tomorrow's my thirtieth birthday.
    One year older, seventeen-and-a-half pounds lighter, morale through the floor, and the weight of the end of the world on my shoulders.

DAY 28: One look at the imperious calendar on my desk and I burst into tears.
    Thirty years old.
    Incredibly, this releases something inside me: crying is a tonic.
    I slip on a dress, push open the front door, and set off for a walk.

DAY 29: Today, same as yesterday, I submerge myself in the forest. It's a glorious day, surprisingly warm for the time of year. The birds haven't resumed their singing (are they even alive still?) but nature seems to be at peace. I walk for hours, my head almost empty of thoughts, watching. Uprooted trees line the path. I have a feeling they were here before, though I can't be sure. The Doubs — green one minute, blue the next — appears to be flowing the wrong way. To be sure I toss out a few twigs, which eddy around and then vanish.

P.S. I've finished the last jar of courgettes. Time to start on the tins.

DAY 30: My steps always lead me back to the same place. I skirt along the main road on the Swiss side of the border, cross over into France at La Rasse, then head back in the opposite direction – past the narrow channel of water, the little peninsula, the scree, the two islets — until I reach La Guêpe.
    La Guêpe was the old glassworks, which today survives only as a clearing in the trees and a concrete slab.
    This is why I moved here, this patch of wild grass by the river, with its memories of sprawling childhood picnics and chorusing frogs.
    It was one of our family hiking destinations, my favourite by far.
    When I was asked once, during therapy, to imagine my safe place, La Guêpe leapt to mind. I pictured myself lying spreadeagled on the grass, my head in the shadow of a large tree and my feet bathed in sunlight.
    We camped here once, you and me, a few years back. Dreaming of the day when, perhaps, we'd be able to move out here permanently.
    Returning to these old haunts, knowing that nobody's watching me, I play like a child — growling like a motorbike down the narrow paths, riding an imaginary horse on the scree, tightrope walking along an ancient tree trunk, laying siege to the islets.

DAY 31: I wake up in a half-decent mood and start a fire in the kitchen stove. Once the embers have formed a dense bed, I place a grate on top and set some water on to boil. Teatime. The simple action floods me with joy — my first hot drink in a month!

A month in which I've lived off pickled vegetables, tinned tuna, cereal and biscuits. High time to ring the changes!

I roll up my sleeves (literally) and get to work, laying out my remaining provisions on the kitchen table: miscellaneous spices, assorted teas, coffee, hot chocolate, cocoa powder, flour, sugar, three cartons of milk, another of coconut milk, three packets of muesli, two of lentils, two more of rice, three of pasta, a tin of chopped tomatoes, one of artichokes, another of chickpeas, fifteen jars of jam, three of honey, a sack of potatoes, three bottles of cordial, seven of white wine, and one of whisky.

I pin the list to the wall, then arrange the supplies in the cupboard in order of expiry date. Everything fits across two shelves. If I'm disciplined, I should have enough to last another month.

During the exercise, I catch myself humming.

DAY 32: Like yesterday, the day before yesterday and the two days before that, I walk out to La Guêpe. I could almost make the journey with my eyes closed, my soles moulding glove-like to the bumpy terrain. The breeze is gentle.

As I pass La Rasse on my way back, a memory stops me in my tracks. In before times, a few dogs used to keep guard here, snarling and barking at every passer-by. Where are they now? Cautiously I approach their enclosure; the gates are ajar, the cages empty. The knowledge that the beasts are roaming free, perhaps restored to their feral state, isn't reassuring. I'm about to turn back when a sound makes me start. Clucking. Despite the fence having been flattened, two hens have lingered in the yard. The birds have the skeletal look of mad drunkards. I spot a packet of feed and sprinkle a generous portion onto the ground. They hurry over as fast as their staggering legs can manage.

What a treat it would be to have fresh eggs!

DAY 37: For the past few days I've been sticking to a strict routine.

- 8.:00 a.m.: wake up
- 8:15 a.m.: egg duty!
- 8:30 a.m.: build fire
- 9:00 a.m.: breakfast (muesli with a dash of hot water; tea)
- 9:30 a.m.: chop firewood
- 10:00 a.m.: walk
- 11:00 a.m.: make flatbread dough
- 12:00 p.m.: lunch (lentils or rice)
- 1:00 p.m.: read; cook flatbreads
- 3:00 p.m.: walk
- 5:00 p.m.: jigsaw or sudoku
- 7:00 p.m.: supper (bread and jam)
- 8:00 p.m.: read by the fire
- 9:30 p.m.: bedtime

P.S. I only went and carted the hens back to Maison-Monsieur! I made for La Rasse armed with a big metal lampshade, then spent two hours cajoling them into my DIY cage (abetted by much chicken feed and tongue-clicking). The return journey was so farcical it's a mighty relief nobody was around to witness it.

DAY 38: As the days go by, the prospect of actually making the trip to La Chaux-de-Fonds seems increasingly remote. I have two opposing theories:

1. The city is ruined, its populace disease-riddled, insurgent or straight-up obliterated.
2. The city is fine, its populace is fine, everything is fine.

Both hypotheses are equally unsettling.

P.S. I dug the old canoe out of the shed. You should have seen me this morning, slicing along the Doubs crooning the soundtrack from *Pocahontas*! After the first bend, beyond that stretch of red trees (which look just as shrivelled even in springtime), I swear I spotted a heron.

DAY 39: The searing frustration, the all-consuming feeling of powerlessness, has now subsided. So what if commissions and interviews are off the agenda?
    At least I'm not drowning in emails, deadlines and stress anymore. Could the end of the world be a blessing in disguise?

P.S. I thought catching a trout would be a cinch. Tie some string to an old awl, spear an earthworm onto the hooked end, and hey presto! What a supreme waste of time. All that effort — trawling the garden for a worm, impaling said worm (with my eyes screwed shut and grimacing), selecting a spot with suitable fishy potential, launching my homespun line a few inches from the bank — only to traipse back empty-handed, four hours later.

DAY 40: Every day I'm confronted afresh by my own cluelessness. I haven't the faintest idea how to start an allotment, incapable as I am of naming a single plant growing in the garden. I've spectacularly failed in each of my trout fishing attempts, and was no more successful at mending the wobbly chair in the living room (it ended up as firewood). And after picking what I mistakenly believed to be wild garlic, I was sick all night.

If I'd been shrewder or more far-sighted, or just better organised, I'd have swotted up on this stuff a long time ago. I wouldn't have been here cobbling together scraps of information – a quick google and a few printouts would have equipped me with a complete survival guide.

And yet, if the internet miraculously returned, scrolling through my recent browser history, you'd find the following search results: the perfect thirtieth birthday present (a La Semeuse coffee machine), my own name (call it writerly self-absorption), Episode 5 of *Jane the Virgin*, the latest book releases from Editions d'Autre Part, the *Bridget Jones* soundtrack, and the Koqa Beatbox official website (don't even ask).

DAY 42: After my serial fishing failures, I decide to hunt the house for anything that, however tenuously, might patch up my knowledge and make daily life easier.

I mastermind an elaborate plan of attack, from basement to attic.

I spend all morning exploring the basement by candlelight, with illuminating results. The unexplored mess left behind by the previous tenants turns out to be a trove of wonders. I emerge with five jars of gherkins, a crate of beer, twenty mysterious tins (contents TBC), another sack of potatoes, bike rims, a few tools, two batteries, one riding helmet and a ski suit.

DAY 43: I found an old Discman!

I full-on screamed when I spotted it tucked in a box in the loft. My hands were shaking when I unzipped the case. The batteries had rusted with age (it must be what, ten, fifteen years old minimum?) and extracting them left my fingers caked in brown powder. After a blow on the springs, I bunged in some new ones and set about choosing between my three-strong teenage CD collection. Decision quickly made, I adjusted the headphones over my ears, then wept as the intro to 'Lady Marmalade' began to play.

DAY 44: I'm still buzzing at this mini-miracle! For over a month, the only music in my life has been the sound of the wind and the crackle of the wood-burner. I know I should be saving batteries, but despite noble intentions and pre-emptive measures (e.g. burying the Discman in the forest), I can't resist blasting out *Moulin Rouge* one more time.

DAY 45: I feel horribly wistful. It must be all that *Moulin Rouge*, the mirage of nothing having changed. Suddenly I'm craving things from *before*.

If the world flipped back to how it was (even for a day) I would love to:

- throw a huge party with everyone I know, and dance until dawn
- turn on every light in the house, then admire the spectacle from across the riverbank
- take an endless scalding hot shower
- order pizza
- board a train
- hear your voice
- go to the cinema
- eat a flavoured yoghurt (chestnut, preferably)
- wander the city after dark

SURVIVOR

* be sent a funny video
* receive a parcel through the post
* hear the doorbell ring
* stuff myself with fruit

I wish I'd never touched that old Discman.

DAY 48: Today marks exactly a year since we moved to Maison-Monsieur. As far as we were concerned, everything was A-MAZING: the view, the Doubs, the garden, the wood heating, the sense of space, the silence, the isolation.

What a joke!

Now that I'm actually forced to chop wood, weed the garden, tend crops, botch my way through successive attempts at fishing, the notion of 'back to nature' has taken on a whole new meaning.

Now that I never receive emails, texts, phone calls or letters, never check the RTS news website and have no idea what's happening six miles up the road, I've understood the true meaning of 'isolation' too.

Now that the roads are empty of traffic, the birds have stopped singing, and the Discman has breathed its last, 'silence' holds no secrets for me either.

And none of it is all it was cracked up to be.

DAY 49: I caught my first trout!

I cooked it over the fire with a sprig of dill, a glug of white wine and some potatoes. Heaven on a plate!

The feat was all thanks to Julien Baillod, a little-known writer who lived around here about a hundred years ago. 'Fish,' he observes, 'often congregate at the foot of waterfalls, close to rocks.

They are lured by all that glistens.'

I made for La Rasse to set up my tackle further downstream, just beyond the waterfall under the bridge. After casting my line, I rippled a spoon through the wavelets to create reflections. Next thing I knew, there was a tug on my rod. I was so shocked I let go of the line and had to restart the whole process from scratch.

DAY 50: When we moved here a year ago, I was brimming with plans. I would swim in the Doubs every morning, go mushroom picking, read my book by the fire, learn about permaculture, take long walks, write a novel.

I went for the odd dip in the heat of summer, but seldom dived into a book. I managed a few walks within a two-mile radius, without ever foraging for mushrooms. I barely wrote a word, claiming I didn't have the time − I had admin to wade through, chores to tick off, people to see.

Since the world ended, I've never read, walked, worked or written so much in my life.

P.S. Not a day goes by − not an hour, even − when the question doesn't occupy my mind. What are they going through right now, my family? My friends? I have tried repeatedly to suppress the train of thought, scared my heart will falter, explode, implode, wither, melt away.

DAY 51: Here's a question I've been chewing over: do I have the right to keep laughing, singing, swimming, masturbating, when the world is collapsing around me?

Today, once and for all, I decide the answer is YES.

DAY 52: Every evening at dusk I've taken to visiting the little island — well, peninsula — that sits a stone's throw from the house, scything the Doubs in two. The grass is improbably vivid, with a peppermint scent. Lying in the middle of it, I work through what my old drama teacher called 'beauty exercises': I hone in on a blade of grass, scrutinising its structure; I try to pick out five different smells; I train my attention on a cloud, tracking it until the wispy form blows over or dissolves; I close my eyes, imagining I'm a kite gliding over the river, a tree changing with the seasons, or a butterfly emerging from its cocoon. I recite poems I learnt as a child, trace made-up alphabets in the air, tune in to the lilting song of the breeze.

DAY 53: I suppose everyone lives out the end of the world differently. In the films, the characters either go to ground, loiter around old supermarkets, or lose themselves in a frenzy of love and alcohol.

Meanwhile, I'm bumbling along fishing, growing tomatoes and caring for a couple of hens. Other than that, my apocalypse days are spent sleeping, bread-making, walking, reading and redoing the same jigsaw again and again.

When I put it like that (ignoring the constant crushing sensation in my chest), it almost sounds like a holiday...

P.S. If everyone's end of the world is different, what would yours be like? Whenever I'm assailed by dark thoughts, I picture you living it up in your teenage apocalypse — partying, drinking, kissing, laughing until your lungs give out.

DAY 54: Each day I venture a little further, discovering new paths, unexplored clearings and abandoned cabins. Sometimes I walk for hours, without ever encountering another soul.

This landscape never ceases to delight and enthral me. The patter of raindrops on the Doubs, the smell of damp earth, the sight of rotting tree stumps, the spongy rocks, the green blush of spring leaves. Every so often, I pause on the sandy banks, sink to my knees, and watch the world shimmering on the surface of the water.

I've set myself the goal of identifying one new plant per day. My *Larousse Illustrated Guide to Wild, Edible and Medicinal Plants* – the only reference book I own – is always in my bag, primed to be consulted with utmost reverence. So far, my cuttings include camomile, angelica, plantain, meadowsweet, navelwort and dandelions.

I'll be forever grateful to my grandmother for giving me the book as a tenth birthday present, a gift whose true worth I sorely underestimated at the time.

DAY 55: Some of my proudest achievements:

- I've learnt to chop wood into even-sized logs
- my flatbreads stay soft for several days
- I smashed my own trout-fishing record (three corkers in a four-hour session!)
- I've harvested enough dandelions for a good four or five salads, and ground up jarfuls of wild garlic pesto
- I've rigged up a natural refrigerator on the bed of the Doubs
- the hens are still alive and laying (albeit erratically)
- my tomatoes are growing (I think)
- my weather forecasts are increasingly accurate
- I've read my way round half the books in the house (including some pretty out-there ones the previous tenants left behind...)
- I've improvised a bathtub from an old laundry container
- thanks to my judicious rationing, I've still enough supplies to hold out for a few weeks yet

DAY 56: On returning home from my island, I sense something has shifted.

Changes: the grass has been trodden down where it wasn't before; the gravel's in a different pattern on the ground. I quicken my pace. Is that a tyre mark on the driveway? My heart pounds in my chest. Wasn't the garden gate shut when I left?

The evidence piles up to mountainous proportions. My tomato plants have been ravaged. The hens' throats have been slit. The intruder has plundered the log store, kicked in the front door. Inside the floor is filthy. Every cupboard ransacked. The whole place has been turned upside down, reduced to mounds of broken glass, scraps of fabric, paper and wood, streaks of piss.

DAY 57: The world has caved in all over again. The fight crushed out of me.

DAY 58: The fucker that trashed my home didn't leave me completely high and dry. Swaddled in a second skin of blankets, I lay out my remaining provisions on the kitchen table and assess the damage. A few spices, some rice, two unlabelled tins, a jar of tomato sauce. But that's it.

How the hell am I supposed to survive on that?

DAY 59: What drives a person to DO something like this? I was just starting to get used to things, to enjoy it, even... Suddenly I'm back to square one. Worse, I can't help but think that everything that's happened so far is just a taster of horrors to come. As though I've been playing at the apocalypse like you might play at doctors and nurses or a teddy bear's picnic.

What now? How do I come back from this?

Even in the middle of an apocalypse, no, ESPECIALLY in the middle of an apocalypse, it's obscenely selfish to rock up and wreck someone else's life. And for what? A few tins and some logs. Senseless, and cruel.

DAY 61: I can't bear to stay any longer in this life, in this body.

An urge to sail free, to escape the void inside me.

DAY 62: Thanks to that bastard:

✺ I'm cold (make that freezing)
✺ I feel panicky in my own home
✺ I jump at the slightest noise
✺ I can't stop shaking
✺ I've barred the front door with two chests of drawers
✺ I've stopped going out
✺ I'm not eating
✺ I wake up at 5:00 a.m.
✺ I'm losing my mind: I enter a room, then have no idea what I'm doing there

DAY 63: I don't recognise my reflection in the mirror: the gnarled frame, protruding hips and shoulder blades, hollow cheeks. I'm so thin I should feel feather-light, yet I no longer have any sense of my own body.

DAY 64: I'm desperately trying to reconnect with my body. To restore some life to things. I hurl myself up and down the stairs, four at a time, until there's no breath left in me. Despite the exertions, my muscles remain anaesthetised, without the merest ache or twinge.

I get a fire roaring in the stove and place two stones on top. While they're warming, I grab the Japanese tatami mat, lay it in front of the flames, then stretch my naked form along it. I slide the burning stones across my skin, over my arms, stomach, breasts and thighs, under the souls of my feet.

It tingles a bit. The sensation isn't unpleasant.

DAY 65: You might think the expression 'hit rock bottom' fitting: a deep lake, with my body sinking down and down before colliding with the muddy floor. Yet it doesn't ring true to me.

If I had to coin a metaphor, plaster an image to what I'm experiencing, I would say I've reached the heart. The process has taken its toll, sapping me of my flesh, breath, tears, energy, certainty. But by digging away, by drilling down to my deepest depths, I've uncovered something elemental.

I can almost see it, this heart which isn't my heart exactly, but something close to it — a core: a white-hot ball tiny enough to cup in my palm, so bright it takes my breath away.

DAY 66: Unable to focus on a book, I retreat to my old comics. I don't process all the words, or look at all the pictures, but for a few seconds I do manage to forget reality.

I have this dream where the intruder returns in the night. I hear the door creak open, footsteps on the stairs. I know instinctively it can only be him. I leap out of bed, grab my candlestick and wait, concealed behind my bedroom door. Then I glimpse the form in the mirror. The intruder is a bear. Or rather, a woman — a huge, ferocious woman — cloaked in a bearskin. I don't breathe. Then, as she enters the room, I slam down the candlestick with all my might. Her skull splinters with a deathly crack.

    I wake up grinning.

DAY 67: Despite the intruder's best efforts:

※ I still crack up laughing at my Garulfo comics
※ I sing in the mornings
※ I feel strong again

DAY 68: I resolve to assemble the IKEA chair that's been loitering in the corner of my bedroom, still in its original packaging.

    A pretty redundant exercise. It would be more productive to mend the cupboard that was smashed by The Ogress (as I've christened her), or sweep the remaining wreckage off the floor, chop some wood, maybe clean the water tank that's been leeching sediment for the past few days.

    Hey-ho. It feels good to build something new.

DAY 69: I inch open the door and peek outside. The coast seems clear. I bolt out into the garden, retrieve as many logs as my arms can carry, hurry back the way I came, slam the door behind me, then collapse in the living room. I spend the afternoon pressed to the window, scanning the perimeter. Total stillness.

    The Ogress's existence has forced me to re-evaluate. I've drawn some divergent conclusions:

1. I'm not the only survivor. Human life goes on, to some degree, which is surely reason to be cheerful?
2. Right on my doorstep there's someone who (out of desperation, or just plain twattishness) had the nerve to break into my home and turn the place over. Not such a cheery thought.
3. The Ogress expressly chose MY house. The four neighbouring buildings (including the restaurant) escaped scot-free. This naturally makes me feel a touch paranoid.

The scariest part of all is that I've no way of knowing if The Ogress will be back.

DAY 70: Flinging open windows. Tossing shards of glass into a bin-bag. Sweeping like a woman possessed. Scrubbing the floor. Airing my duvet. Rearranging the furniture. Burning incense.

Once all that's done I lay three logs in the stove, light a fire and set some water boiling. I tip half into my Thermos flask and pour the rest into a washbowl. Then, plunging a flannel into the scalding liquid, I scour myself from head to toe.

Day fades into night. For the first time since The Ogress descended, sleep comes easily.

DAY 71: I don't know whether my brain cells blew at the same time as the electricity or if my moral compass was somehow diverting me: I live next door to a RESTAURANT (duh!). And what's more, I have the key to it... I guess they won't be needing it.

Euphoria quashes my reservations. I mean, if they've vanished anyway. I scan the vicinity from the front step, then close the door behind me and leg it to the building next door.

My eyes can't take it in. I'd forgotten that such an abundance of food could exist. Admittedly, the fruit has all rotted and the frozen stuff has melted or mouldered, but I reckon what's left could sustain me for months, years even. There's flour, sugar, cereal, long-lasting vegetables, tins, jars, jars and more jars, plus all the wine you could ever wish for.

In an apocalypse film you'd see me popping open the champagne, rolling in the crates of potatoes and whooping while sinking my arms into huge sacks of flour.

In real life I remain rooted to the spot, gawping.

I leave empty-handed.

DAYS 72, 73, 74, 75, 76 AND 77: Every day I make one round trip, bringing back only what I deem 'strict essentials':

- Tuesday: flour (a 10kg sack) and a lighter
- Wednesday: potatoes and violet syrup
- Thursday: tea, chocolate, a VCR player, batteries, a CD (nothing but classical! In the end, Rachmaninov gets to rule my apocalypse soundwaves)
- Friday: loo roll
- Saturday: cabbage and carrots
- Sunday: toothpaste, soap, chewing gum, pens, account books

Daily life is peaceful. I only leave the house to make this same trip. I while away the remaining hours cooking, reading the same comics over and over, humming Schubert, drinking tea, napping.

DAY 78: It's a tiny detail that does it: a tyre track on the driveway. I stalk around the mark then scrub it out with my foot, harder and harder until every last trace of The Ogress is erased. I feel a surge of invincibility. Time to reclaim my territory! For a second, I toy with the idea of urinating along the perimeter. A vestige of modesty stops me. Instead, I light an incense stick and weave an invisible loop around the house, garden and driveway, bellowing incantations. I look like a complete idiot.

Fired up, I plonk myself down on a deckchair and scrawl insult-laden missives to The Ogress. Later, I'll watch them perish in the flames.

DAY 79: My fear has burnt away, and from the embers a searing rage has erupted. The inferno rips through everything in its path, reigniting old grudges:

- Against my driving test examiner, for failing me at my first attempt for being 'a bit too cautious'
- against my teenage best friend, for not jumping to my defence when the mate of a mate declared I was a 'wannabe grunger' and sloshed beer all over my corduroy trousers.
- against my German exchange partner, for abandoning me by the roadside when my bike got a puncture.
- against my parents, for not having nurtured my ambition of becoming a footballer
- against my friendship group, for saddling me with the labels of 'shy', 'lazy' and 'scatty'
- against the friends who've gone on to start families, for demoting me to second fiddle
- against anyone who outshines me at anything (whatever the task may be)
- against you, for this ache that won't go away

DAY 80: If you were here, the end of the world would be bearable.

The veg plot would be resplendent with tomatoes, salad leaves, fennel, carrots and every crop imaginable. You'd have no trouble snooping out a prime fishing spot and stringing together a net, and without us lifting a finger, it would be teeming with trout. You'd find an ingenious way of fixing the leaky water tank. You'd dream up some inspired solution to revive the electricity, harnessing the power of the sun, wind or water, or just by pedalling away on a bike.

With you here, apocalypse life would have a fizz of adventure. The thrill of the unknown, the comfort of the familiar. We'd sleep under the stars, construct bridges, skim stones and play cards. We'd read novels aloud, plot maps of the surrounding area, drink beer... we'd dare to journey as far as La Chaux-de-Fonds.

But if you were here, would the world even have ended in the first place?

DAY 81: Things I wish we'd had the chance to do (once or for the umpteenth time) together:

- see Japan in springtime
- celebrate St Patrick's Day in Ireland
- finish off the last series of *Naruto*
- eat crêpes
- go to a Proclaimers gig
- play ping-pong
- live in Berlin
- go camping
- drink beer in a pub
- celebrate our twentieth anniversary
- paraglide
- sail along a river in a barge
- walk down the street hand in hand

DAY 82: It takes a trifling chain of events to set my inner storm whirling again. Struggling to open the still-wonky cupboard, chopping some wood, inexpertly repotting the tomatoes, and then, as I'm coming back from my island, glimpsing what looks from afar like an ogre, a wheel, a vehicle, a silhouette, your silhouette.

DAY 83: I could start a fire or flood the banks of the Doubs with this rage. I've lost all sense of how to channel it and against what — or whom. For want of a better alternative, I plunge into the river, letting the cold needle every pore of me, and swim until my body is warm once more.

DAY 88: Mental note (8:23 a.m.):
    Fuck you.
Mental note (12:33 p.m.):
    Sayonara, sucker!
Mental note (3:43 p.m.):
    Goodbye for real?

DAY 91: My emotions are all over the place. Just when I thought the anger, doubt and grief were done with. I fall asleep unsure what state I'll wake up in the following morning; I drift through the days not knowing what my mood will do from one hour to the next. It's exhausting.

I wish there were an end-of-the-world textbook. Having always been a conscientious and assiduous student, I'd give my right arm to have someone set me apocalypse homework. I'd tick off the checklist in my weekly planner, then sleep like a baby.

※ Monday: shock ✓
※ Tuesday: loss ✓

- ✷ Wednesday: doubt ✓
- ✷ Thursday: anger ✓
- ✷ Friday: sadness
- ✷ Saturday: breather
- ✷ Sunday: rest

DAY 92: I wish I could wake up from this nightmare.

DAY 93: *Dear future me,*
In 2019, you lived through an apocalypse. It was incredibly brutal, unexpected, unfair and upsetting. Overnight, you found yourself alone in the eye of the storm. All around you, everything looked the same, yet had changed beyond recognition.
You had to pick yourself up, rebuild your nest, forge a daily routine, hone new skills and reconnect with old 'passions'.
By the time you read this, you'll be older (for sure!), wiser (possibly), and at peace (I hope).
This is what I wish for you, future me: walks in the forest, jigsaws, mugs of steaming tea, time to read, stimulating encounters, log fires, parties that last long into the night, music, birdsong and so much else that's too fabulous to fathom right now! In your moments of doubt, fear or anger, remember that somewhere inside you, there's always a heart beating bright (and that you still burst out laughing every time you read Garulfo*).*
Take care of yourself (of us!)

I write this letter on my best notepaper, roll it up, slip it into a bottle that I tuck in my rucksack, then stride out to La Guêpe.
 I feel taller, like I've been stretched by a few inches. As I pass the water, the red trees, the scree and the islets once more, my body

drinks in the passage of time. 'The last time I came here, the weight bearing down on me seemed heavier than it does today...' The realisation fills me with astonishment and delight.

When I reach La Guêpe, I kneel at the foot of my tree. The wild grass is almost armpit-high. As I'm about to cast adrift the bottle, my hand wavers. I know my trepidation is stupid. I've sent hundreds of email attachments over the years without a thought for the environmental impact, yet here I am dithering — because these words have a material existence.

DAY 93: *Dear stranger,*

If you're reading this message, that means the Doubs has swept my bottle all the way to you, a fellow survivor of this apocalypse.

What's your life like, dear stranger? I'd love to know, so here's my address: 17 Côtes-du-Doubs. If you get the chance (and you're not an ogre(ss)), do come and say hello!

All the best.

DAY 96: *Hi stranger,*

I have so many questions for you! Do you have any tips on growing tomatoes? (Mine are refusing to get any bigger!) Do the birds sing where you are? Could I start a rice paddy on the banks of the Doubs? What are the long-term effects of a planet without electricity?

It would be fantastic to meet you!

All the best.

P.S. I feel weirdly like my ten-year-old self again, sending off letters to my Swiss-German pen pal.

JULIE GUINAND

DAY 99: *Hello stranger,*
What was your life like before? Did you buy strawberries out of season? Did you watch Netflix? Did you have strong opinions on the final season of Game of Thrones? *Did you ever forget to vote? Were you mad on politics? Did you listen to La Chanson du Dimanche's latest hit every Sunday? Were you a gamer? Did you dream of having your own house, a dog, a family... or did you already have all that? Did you sometimes despair when you listened to the news? Did you plan to do the grand rail tour of Switzerland one day? Did you watch TV sport? Were you wistful for the days of MSN Messenger? Did you dream of printing your own POGs and sparking a Gen Z milk cap revival? Did you hanker for a digital detox from time to time? Were you happy with your life as it was?*
All the best.

P.S. *Personally, my answers would be: no — yes — yes — no — yes — yes — no — no — no — yes — not really — no (except tennis) — no — no (sadly, I didn't own one of those marvellous machines) — yes — yes.*

DAY 100: *Dearest stranger,*
This letter will be my last.
I look forward to you visiting me at 17 Côtes-du-Doubs. Don't you think the end of the world would be more fun with two of us?
All the best.
I can't stop daydreaming that the bottle will drift its way to you, and that, one glorious day, I'll open the door to find you waiting.

DAY 115: Thank god I'd printed out a draft. After filling two fat notebooks with letters, poems, lullabies, lists and plot finales for Netflix series that were interrupted mid-season, I resume writing my novel. The one that was meant to write itself — or so I thought when I moved here. The one that, since the world ended, has ground to a deadly halt.

DAY 116: I've just re-read the start of my novel, twice. It struck me as amateurish, irrelevant, way off-beam. Like somebody else had written it.

Strangely enough, this doesn't much dampen my motivation. The inky pages even yield a kind of comfort – if I'd been a photographer, architect, mechanic, geographer, engineer, pilot, astronaut, paramedic, baker, brewer, IT technician or whatever else, my work would have been profoundly changed, jeopardised even. I feel lucky to have an *apocalypti-compatible* vocation!

That said, it would have been handier to have been an electrician...

DAY 117: I'd like to write a book that makes sense in the current circumstances.

Ideally, it would feature:

- humour
- magic
- practical tips
- a happy ending (?)
- a young, strong heroine (think Moana, or Chihiro from *Spirited Away*)
- short musings on life (but nothing too heavy)
- riddles to solve (?)

DAY 120: I've restarted from scratch.

It's all over the place, veering off in all directions, but I've never written with such relish.

DAY 141: I knew the world around me wasn't perfect. I found it infuriating, dispiriting, distressing at times. I would have liked it to be fairer, greener, more just, governed with greater respect and wisdom. Yet I'd never have wished to be born in another age, or on a different planet. I felt at home.

When the electricity died, I fixated on things lost: hot showers, the hum of the computer, the bleeping of my alarm.

Now I feel like I've reached an epiphany. Even before the end of it, the world around me was in constant flux. When I was born, The internet didn't exist. I was twenty-two when I watched my first Netflix series. Some of those technological changes happened gradually, others were more dramatic, but none of them had any lasting impact on my well-being — not in a fundamental sense.

For the first time in four months, I'm starting to ask myself whether the end of this world might just hail the start of a new one... and might I actually be *happy* there?

P.S. I've finished the first draft of my 'novel'. It's unlike anything I've encountered before, and I'm incapable of assessing its literary merit.

DAY 142: I'm on my island when the birds start singing again. The sound is so deafening I have to clamp my hands to my ears.

Propelled by instinct, I leap up, hare off home and flick the nearest light switch. As if there were some logical correlation; as if the birds were powered by electricity too.

Nothing happens. It's a relief.

DAY 150: It's been five months since my reading lamp died. Five months since the electricity tripped. Five months since the world as I knew it disappeared.

Today I feel calmer, like the worst is behind me.

DAY 151: On my way back from Biaufond, I run into a badger. He stares at me, frozen in the middle of the path, then shakes his snout before vanishing between the trees. I'm left gawping in stupefaction.

The moment I get home I make for *The Big Book of Symbols*, which was given to me by a friend as a kind of in-joke.

BADGER – *strength, dynamism, persistence. Totem of the healing process. A person endowed with the strength of a badger can draw on the animal's stubbornness to heal herself. The badger shows us that we must deploy our aggressive energy to move forwards, though not at the expense of others. The creature is a symbol of inner balance.*

DAY 152: I have been thinking about the badger with his stripy snout and gentle gaze.

Maybe it is time to move on.

DAY 153: I can feel the winds of adventure whipping up inside me, a yearning for something else that blows stronger by the hour.

My mind tries to beat back the urge. The most rational course of action would be to carry on the way I am. I've enough food, firewood, water and reading material to hold out for a good while yet, enough to see me through summer and winter. My log chopping skills are now (almost) pro standard; I can build a fire, catch fish, identify a few dozen plants and fill all the empty hours in the day. Setting off into the unknown would be risky.

But that's not the only thing. A crazy idea holds me back: the thought that one day, you might come home.

DAY 154: OK. I'm going.

DAY 155: I'm taking my time over this expedition, planning everything down to the last detail. I place my rucksack on the kitchen table and tape a sheet of paper down next to it: time to write my packing list. I don't want to overburden myself, nor to overlook anything essential. I mentally divvy up the house – garden, kitchen, living room, bedroom, bathroom – and assign myself one room per day.

DAY 156 – The Garden: Since the world ended, the garden has become the hub of my existence – my living room, kitchen, utility room and bathroom rolled into one. Whenever it's not raining (and I'm not paralysed by the fear of The Ogress reappearing), I spend most of my time outside: chopping wood, tending the fire, cooking food, heating water, doing my laundry, having a wash, and reading for hours on end.

306 days before the power cut:

The fire has been crackling since noon. Silhouetted figures come and go around the fireside, amid aromas of peppers, chicken and melted cheese. Various groups form and disperse as the afternoon wears on. A few people start up a game of pétanque on the gravel; hoots of laughter erupt from beneath the fiery red bows of the Japanese maple; pop! a bottle is uncorked to a theatrical chorus of 'ahhhh's.

An intrepid little band decides to take a dip in the Doubs. As clothes are strewn higgledy-piggledy across the riverbank our toes venture into the river, disturbing the serene world in miniature on its surface. With howls, giggles and whoops, we launch ourselves into the water, thrashing out a few daredevil strokes before retreating to the bank. We shake ourselves off like giddy grasshoppers, swathed in fluffy towels.

Although we were only gone for a few minutes, the party we rejoin is not the same one we left. The guests have traded in their wineglasses for beer, whisky and limoncello. A shisha pipe is being passed from hand to hand, suffusing the air with a heady scent of rose. I allow myself to be rocked into a trance, while my eyes wander in search of you.

Your face is lit in gold and red as you stoke the fire. You catch my gaze, then you smile.

DAY 157 — *The Kitchen*: Unlike the rest of the house, the kitchen has hardly changed since we moved in. The middle of the room is dominated by the huge black island which houses the oven, dishwasher and sink. I decided that cutlery would live in the top drawer and pans in the bottom one. Glasses, mugs and bowls are stacked in the cupboard next to the fridge (now bare and out of action) and non-perishables go in the little cupboard underneath. Even though there's nothing to be found simmering, boiling, freezing or whirring away in here anymore, I felt it vital to preserve this once logical order of things.

First night after the power cut:
I open the fridge. Occupying a good half of the lower shelf

presides a magnificent custard tart. To be safe, I check the sell-by date. It expired more than a week ago. 'To hell with it,' I sputter to myself, stuffing down a sizeable wedge, 'I can't resist'.

DAY 158 — The Living Room: The house has two reception rooms, one leading off the front hallway and a second upstairs. The first is vast, spanning almost the footprint of the building. I'd set up my office in there, fancying that in such surroundings my future bestseller would all but write itself.

When the apocalypse hit, I gradually abandoned that downstairs room. It was too big for me, a pain to heat. I began by lugging the armchair and blankets upstairs, then relocated the bookcase and office equipment. I left the door onto the hallway ajar though, so I could still enjoy the view from the downstairs loo.

The upstairs living room is, after the garden, the place where I've spent the most time since the world ended. Giving as it does onto the kitchen, from there I can keep an eye on everything – the stove, the wood supply, the food situation, the bathroom and my books.

54 days before the power cut:

'Luna, I've just clocked off at the Ministry of Magic and I'm heading for the 15:01 Hogwarts Express. Fancy fixing us a bite to eat?'

I put the kettle on, a spoonful of Earl Grey in the teapot and stick an extra log in the stove. I cut up an apple, arrange the slices daintily on a plate and add a sprinkle of cinnamon, then carry everything over to the coffee table along with a packet of biscuits. I hear the distinctive crunch of your footsteps on the gravel. 'Helloooo!' you call, pushing open the front door, hanging up your coat and climbing the stairs. You greet me with a smile.

I lay my head on your shoulder, keeping it nestled for a moment in the crook of your neck. 'So, where are you up to with the book?' you ask, pouring out the tea. 'Harry's just been picked for the Triwizard

Tournament. You?' 'Malfoy's been attacked by the hippogriff. It's only a scratch but he's making a right meal of it...'

The silence, punctuated by the rustle of pages, is periodically broken for just long enough to take a bite of biscuit, gulp down some tea, and kiss one another on the cheek.

DAY 159 — The Bedroom: Ever since The Ogress broke in, my bedroom has had the feel of a cutlery factory: bread knife on the dressing table (flanked by hairbrush and lip balm), steak knife in my underwear drawer, and Swiss Army knife under the bed.

Probably a futile precaution, but it helps stave off the nightmares. 30 days before the power cut:

Sunshine creeps in through the dormer, bathing the bed in light and casting a halo over your tousled hair. The little beam dances from side to side as the breeze ripples through the trees outside.

I pretend I'm a cat, pouncing to catch a ray between my claws. 'What the fuck are you doing?' you grumble. 'I'm a cat,' I reply. 'Purrr!' You stare at me for a moment, unconvinced, then explode with laughter.

DAY 160 — The Bathroom: The bathroom isn't such a soothing place without hot water, so I've mainly steered clear these past few months. I brush my teeth over the sink in the kitchen, and wash in a basin by the stove to save me heaving the dead weight from room to room. I keep the door shut most of the time, only venturing inside if I need to rummage in the medicine cabinet for plasters or tick spray.

One day before the power cut:

I suddenly notice your shampoo bar is missing. 'Hmm,' I think to myself, 'one day — just like that — a guy walks out on his old life, leaving everything except his shampoo. Now, that's what I call an ad campaign.'

DAY 161: I'm all set. My rucksack, groaning at the seams, is propped upright against the front door. I square up to it from the bottom step, where I sit freshly shod for action. I've just finished my farewell tour. A chance to say goodbye to the ghost of you, and a thank you to the walls, stove, sofa, bed and other faithful objects that have made this apocalypse life bearable.

My rucksack slumps down a few inches, scraping the wall as it goes. I take it as my cue to leave. Getting to my feet, I hoist the bag onto my shoulders (Christ, it's heavy!) and adjust the straps. Then, with a final scan around, I push open the door and click it shut behind me.

I lumber along the road, every so often jiggling one deadened shoulder after the other to redistribute the load. I grant myself regular rests — there's no deadline looming over me, no cars, motorbikes or cyclists to contend with, not a single animal in sight.

The uphill leg takes me two hours. It's early afternoon by the time I hit the edge of the forest, where the road forks in two. I freeze at the junction, weighing up my options... After what seems like an age, I dump my rucksack on the tarmac and sit down next to it.

Dusk descends over the landscape, shadowing the junction where my arse is still glued to the tarmac. I won't go any further. I step across the barbed wire fence, deposit my bag, pitch my tent, then head into the forest. Once I've gathered enough wood to start a fire, I perch on a rock and attempt to warm my icy hands. If this were a disaster film, I'd be oozing wild, sensual vibes, like some vampish twenty-first century cowgirl. As it is, I just look like a prat stranded by the side of the road. Having forgotten to pack a grill rack, I try balancing my tin of ravioli between a pair of logs. Eventually, I admit defeat, and gulp down a tepid blend of tomatoey pasta and ash.

DAY 162: It's been raining since this morning. After giving up on the fire, I spend the day holed up in my tent. Around midday, I could have sworn I heard cowbells.

DAY 163: I rise with the sun. The grass is shimmering with dew, mingled with yesterday's raindrops. Thankfully, the heavens finally closed after dark. I blow on the embers until the fire has revived, then set some water to boil. After swallowing down my breakfast of watery muesli, I fold up the tent, stamp out the remaining embers with my right heel and bundle everything into my rucksack. Adjusting the straps over my shoulders, I clamber back over the barbed wire fence and set off, without thinking, towards La Chaux-de-Fonds. I wind along the Biaufond road, through the funny patch of countryside that my child self christened 'the chicken trail', past the riding school where I used to have lessons as a teenager, and the buildings where my sister and I would go skateboarding on the sly.

When I reach the edge of the city, I take a deep breath and stop still, gazing out on the new world.

+SVIZRA is a series of eight chapbooks showcasing contemporary writing translated from the four official languages of Switzerland: German, French, Italian and Romansh. In giving equal visibility to each of the four languages, **+SVIZRA** offers a range of Swiss writing never before seen in English from a diverse group of some of the best authors living and working in Switzerland today, including National Literature Prize winning Anna Ruchat, Iraqi exile Usama Al-Shahmani and treasured Romansh author, Rut Plouda.

+SVIZRA is the result of Strangers Press' latest exciting collaboration with an international group of authors, translators, publishers, designers and editors, all made possible by generous funding from Pro Helvetia.

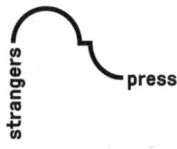

Supported By

University of East Anglia

NORWICH
UNIVERSITY
OF THE ARTS